PRINCESS MINNIE

LADY DAISY

CAPTAIN PETE

CLARABELLE

THE BEAGLE BOYS

For information regarding permission, write to:
Disney Licensed Publishing,
114 Fifth Avenue, New York, New York 10011

0-7172-7762-3

Printed in the U.S.A.
First printing, November 2004

DISNEY'S

MICKEY · DONALD · GOOFY

The Three Musketeers

SCHOLASTIC INC.

New York   Toronto   London   Auckland   Sydney
Mexico City   New Delhi   Hong Kong   Buenos Aires

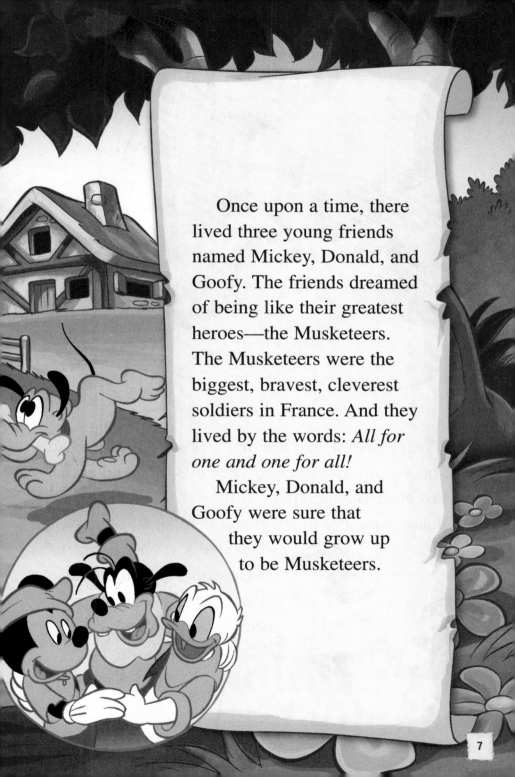

Once upon a time, there lived three young friends named Mickey, Donald, and Goofy. The friends dreamed of being like their greatest heroes—the Musketeers. The Musketeers were the biggest, bravest, cleverest soldiers in France. And they lived by the words: *All for one and one for all!*

Mickey, Donald, and Goofy were sure that they would grow up to be Musketeers.

Years passed, and the three friends still dreamed of becoming Musketeers. They even worked at the Musketeer Headquarters. If they worked hard, then Mickey was sure that Captain Pete, head of the Musketeers, would notice them. Captain Pete did notice them—when a water pipe accidentally broke while he was taking his monthly shower!

When Captain Pete came crashing into the room, he found a disaster. Little Mickey couldn't control the wild pipe. Donald was hiding from the spouting water. Goofy was stuck in a ladder.

"W-w-we were practising our teamwork so we can be good Musketeers," Mickey tried to explain to Captain Pete.

Pete just laughed. He thought Mickey was too small, Donald was a coward, and Goofy was—well, goofy. Pete would never make *them* Musketeers!

Pete quickly left the three friends because he had plans—evil plans! Pete wanted to become king of France. He had his lieutenant, Clarabelle, helping him. Pete had hired the Beagle Boys to kidnap Princess Minnie. Then at the opera the next night, the smallest Beagle Boy would dress like Minnie and announce that Pete was the new king!

Princess Minnie was unaware of
Pete's plan. As she sat in the throne room,
her thoughts were on only one thing—love.

"He loves me, he loves me a lot," Minnie
sighed, plucking petals from a flower.

"Who's the lucky guy?" Daisy, Minnie's lady-in-
waiting, wanted to know.

"Trust me, Daisy. I'll know him when I see him,"
Minnie replied.

Minnie and Daisy went out to the garden. When Princess Minnie paused on the palace steps, the Beagle Boys pushed a safe off the balcony. They just missed the princess!

When Captain Pete found out what had happened, he was furious! "I didn't say 'drop a safe,' I said 'keep her safe,'" he shouted at the bumbling Beagle Boys.

Pete turned to Clarabelle. "Throw these clowns into the pit!"

"No! No! Anything but the pit!" cried the Beagle Boys.
Clarabelle showed them no mercy
and tossed them down. Fortunately,
the pit wasn't very deep.

Then the phone rang. "Princess
Minnie!" a surprised Clarabelle cried.
It seemed Pete wasn't the only one
who was angry.

"I want bodyguards," Princess Minnie told Captain Pete, "Musketeer bodyguards."

Pete knew that *real* Musketeers would interfere with his plan. Luckily, he had an idea.

"Princess, you're in luck. Have I got the men for you," Pete promised, with a sly smile.

Meanwhile, Mickey was trying to cheer up his friends. "I'm sure there's some way we can become real Musketeers. Someday Cap'n Pete's gonna march in here and say—"

"Congratulations," Pete broke in. "You guys have what it takes to be Musketeers!"

The three friends couldn't believe it. Mickey happily shouted, "All for one . . ."

". . . and two for tea," Goofy finished. Okay, so they weren't exactly ready, and that's just what Pete was counting on!

Later, Captain Pete presented his three new Musketeers to Princess Minnie. The princess was smitten with Mickey the instant she saw him.

Pete promised that the Three Musketeers would fight anyone to keep the princess safe.

At that moment, Daisy entered the room, carrying a
tray with a knife and cheese.

"Knife!" shouted Goofy.

"Bad guy!" shouted Donald.

The Three Musketeers tackled Daisy!

Princess Minnie shouted, "Oh! Oh! Stop it!
Drop her!"

Things weren't off to
a great start. . . .

. . . And they were about to get worse! Mickey,
Donald, and Goofy didn't know they were about to
face real bad guys.

Pete had ordered the Beagle Boys to kidnap the
princess. The Beagle Boys were waiting as the Royal
Coach passed by.

The Beagle Boys jumped onto the coach.

"Bad guys!" Donald shouted.

Mickey was ready to fight, but Donald jumped into the coach.

"Get back out there, you coward," Minnie scolded Donald as she pushed him out.

Donald landed in the mud. He watched helplessly as Mickey and Goofy tried to fight off the Beagle Boys.

The kidnappers quickly outwitted Goofy, though. And little Mickey was no match for the big bullies.

23

Soon the Three Musketeers were in the mud. The Beagle Boys made their escape with Princess Minnie and Daisy still in the Royal Coach.

"It's hopeless," said Donald, sighing.

But Mickey wasn't ready to give up. "Pete made us Musketeers, remember?" Mickey reminded his friends. They nodded.

"So we're off to save the princess!" Mickey shouted. The Three Musketeers quickly headed after the coach.

They found the Royal Coach near a deserted tower. But when Mickey and Donald tried to open the tower door, it was stuck.

"Let me give it a go," Goofy said. But he didn't know that Mickey and Donald had been pulling to open the door. So Goofy ran at it as hard as he could. The door swung open and Goofy raced past.

As Goofy ran up the stairs, he accidentally knocked things out of the window. That gave him an idea.

With Mickey and Donald close behind, Goofy managed to knock the kidnappers out of another window and into the river below.

Princess Minnie and Daisy were amazed at Goofy's clever plan. Then the Three Musketeers escorted the ladies back to the palace.

But the danger wasn't over yet. As Goofy stood guard outside Princess Minnie's room, another door creaked open.

"Mickey?" Goofy questioned, seeing a familiar shadow. "Yes, Musketeer Goofy," said a voice. "I am in need of your assistance."

Goofy followed the shadow
out of the palace.

Of course, it wasn't Mickey
at all. Clarabelle had tricked
Goofy into following her. She
quickly had Goofy trapped.

Meanwhile, Donald was patrolling the palace as well. When he spotted the Beagle Boys, he drew his sword.

"Don't move!" Donald shouted bravely. But the Beagle Boys drew their weapons, anyway.

"Wak!" shouted Donald. He ran! Luckily, as he was running and hiding, he discovered Pete's secret plan.

Mickey couldn't believe it when he found Donald hiding. "What's the big idea?" Mickey asked.

Donald quickly explained that Pete had been planning to kidnap Minnie all along.

Mickey couldn't believe it. "But he . . . he made us Musketeers."

"It was all a lie!" shouted Donald.

"Well, lie or no lie, Musketeers don't run from danger," Mickey began. "And as long as we wear these uniforms, neither do we."

That was all Donald needed to hear. He tore off his uniform.

Mickey tried to stop him. "Donald, wait! Together we can stop Captain Pete."

Donald shook his head. "I just can't . . . I'm sorry."

Mickey walked away, alone. He didn't know someone was watching!

"Well, well, well, if it ain't the one Musketeer," Pete said, stepping from the shadows.

Bravely, Mickey faced him. "Captain Pete, by the power vested in me as a Musketeer, I arrest you!"

Pete laughed and with one blow knocked out Mickey!

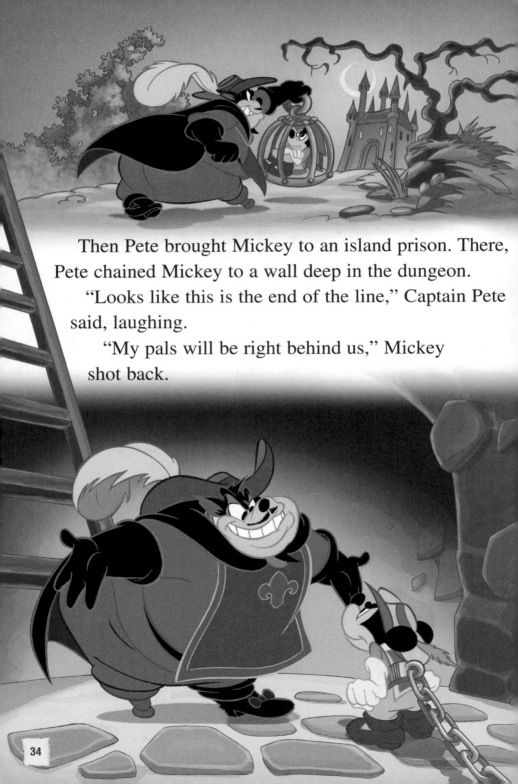

Then Pete brought Mickey to an island prison. There, Pete chained Mickey to a wall deep in the dungeon.

"Looks like this is the end of the line," Captain Pete said, laughing.

"My pals will be right behind us," Mickey shot back.

"Oh, sure. The duck dumped ya, and the goof is getting fitted for a halo," Captain Pete replied. "Face it! You are on your own!"

Pete had to leave for the opera to complete his plan. But as he left, he called to Mickey. "You know, they say the tide comes in faster than horses."

Suddenly water began to pour into the dungeon. Soon it would be flooded.

Mickey wasn't the only one in danger. Clarabelle was about to throw Goofy off a bridge!

But something unexpected had happened. Goofy had fallen in love with Clarabelle! He sang her a love song, and she couldn't resist him!

She told Goofy that Mickey was in great danger. Then as she tried to free Goofy, the bridge railing gave way. Goofy and Clarabelle plunged over the side . . .

. . . and landed in a boat that was being rowed
by Donald!

The boat sank, but everyone made it to the bank of
the river. Goofy knew they had to save Mickey. "It's
all for one and one for all," he reminded Donald.

Donald still didn't feel brave enough to help.

By now, the water in Mickey's cell was rising quickly. Mickey hadn't been able to break free from his chains. Just when it looked as if all hope was lost, Goofy and Donald arrived!

They quickly freed Mickey and got him to safety.

But Mickey wasn't so sure they could save the princess now. "Aw, fellas, we're not even real Musketeers," he said, with a sigh.

"Who says so," Goofy replied. "Donald might be a big chicken, and you're just a little guy, and I ain't no genius. But when the three of us stick together . . ."

". . . we can do anything!" finished Donald.

Mickey stood up. "Musketeers, we've got a princess to save!" The three friends raced off to the opera.

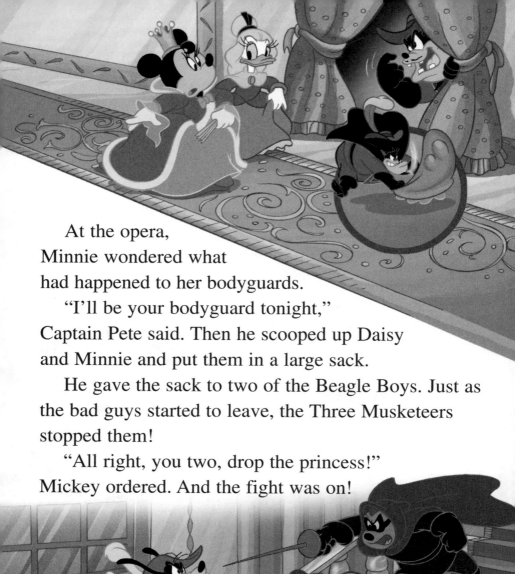

At the opera,
Minnie wondered what
had happened to her bodyguards.

"I'll be your bodyguard tonight,"
Captain Pete said. Then he scooped up Daisy
and Minnie and put them in a large sack.

He gave the sack to two of the Beagle Boys. Just as
the bad guys started to leave, the Three Musketeers
stopped them!

"All right, you two, drop the princess!"
Mickey ordered. And the fight was on!

But were they too late? The smallest Beagle Boy, dressed as Princess Minnie, had gone onstage. "Attention, my loyal subjects," the fake princess announced. "Due to the stress of princessing—I now present your new ruler, King Pete!"

The audience sat in shock as the opera began—and a sword fight erupted onstage!

From his seat, Captain Pete saw the battle and quickly joined in. Mickey had just freed Minnie and Daisy when he had to face Captain Pete alone! Goofy and Donald were too busy with the Beagle Boys to help.

Pete managed to knock Mickey to the ground. "It's all over," Pete said. "And you're all alone."

"Wanna bet?" Mickey said, looking up. Goofy and Donald were on their way! They had just defeated the Beagle Boys backstage. Together, they knocked Captain Pete silly and ended his evil plan.

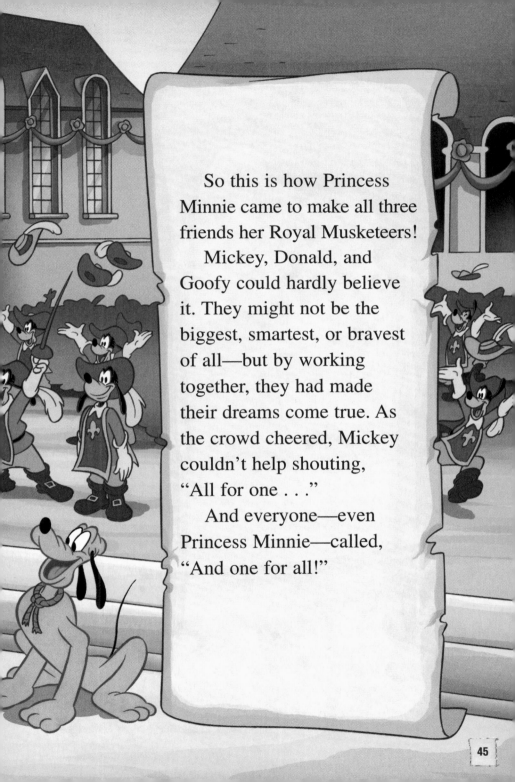

So this is how Princess Minnie came to make all three friends her Royal Musketeers!

Mickey, Donald, and Goofy could hardly believe it. They might not be the biggest, smartest, or bravest of all—but by working together, they had made their dreams come true. As the crowd cheered, Mickey couldn't help shouting, "All for one . . ."

And everyone—even Princess Minnie—called, "And one for all!"